Produced by Kroha Associates, Inc.
Middletown, Connecticut.

Printed in the United States of America.

ISBN 1-56326-115-4

Being Nice Is Better

One sunny Saturday, Minnie and her friends were playing on the swings in the park. They were having a good time taking turns pushing each other, and seeing who could swing the highest.

"Look at me," shouted Daisy. "I can nearly touch the sun!"

"That's because I gave you such a good push," Penny said.

Just then, Becky Matthews walked up to Penny. "I want to swing now. Make Daisy get off!" Becky yelled as she grabbed at the swing. "Don't do that!" Penny said.

"Try and stop me!" Becky answered. She dumped a handful of sand on the back of Penny's head. Minnie and Daisy jumped off the swings.

"Come on, everyone, let's leave!" Minnie said.

"What's the matter — are you chicken?" Becky yelled.

"To my house!" Minnie shouted. The girls ran from the park as fast as they could, and they didn't stop until they reached Minnie's backyard.

"At least Becky can't bother us here," Minnie gasped as they sat down to rest.

"Well, she bothers us everywhere else," Daisy complained. "At the park, at school — she's a big bully!"

"I'm scared of her," Clarabelle whispered.

"I think she likes it when we get scared and run away," Minnie said. "Maybe if we ignore her, she'll stop pestering us."

"I'll try anything!" Penny said. "This is the fourth time this week she's put sand in my hair, and I'm getting tired of washing it!"

At school on Monday, Minnie and her friends tried to ignore Becky, but she acted worse than ever!

First, she pulled the ribbon from Lilly's hair.

Then, during recess, she made fun of Clarabelle's walk. Clarabelle just kept on walking. "Clownabelle, Clownabelle," Becky called after her.

At lunch, Becky cut in front of Penny in the cafeteria line. Penny tried staring at the ceiling and ignoring her, so Becky knocked Penny's milk on the floor.

When Becky dumped Minnie's schoolwork out of her book bag, Minnie didn't say a word — not even when Becky stepped all over the papers!

After school, Becky followed the girls as they walked home.

"What's she going to do now?" Daisy sighed, looking over her shoulder.

"You mean, what are we going to do now?" Penny said. "Ignoring Becky doesn't work at all!"

"It's hard to ignore someone who won't leave you alone," Lilly said.

"Let's go to your house, Minnie, and try to think of another plan," Daisy suggested.

"There must be a way to make Becky stop bullying us!" Minnie said as she made her friends peanut butter and banana sandwiches.

"Let's pour glue in the sandpile," Penny exclaimed. "Then, when Becky tries to throw sand, it'll stick to her and she'll turn into an itchy, scratchy sand person!"

Clarabelle giggled. "We could push her so high in a swing that she gets stuck in a tree!"

"We could make her jump into a big hole full of peanut butter so she'd stick!" Daisy added.

Everyone started to laugh. They laughed so hard that for a minute they forgot to be scared of Becky.

"Being mean to Becky would make us just as mean as she is," Minnie said. "But don't worry, we'll think of something, I'm sure!"

After her friends left, Minnie went outside to call Fifi. Just then Fifi came running up the walk with a big, shaggy dog chasing her!

As Minnie watched, Fifi stopped running and faced the big dog. Her ears and tail stood straight up. She started to bark.

The big dog stopped and stared at Fifi. Fifi barked louder. Then the big dog began to back away. Fifi didn't budge — she just kept on barking. The big dog yelped, and ran away!

After school the next day, Minnie waited for her friends to walk home with her so she could share her idea.

"I can't walk home today, Minnie," Clarabelle said. "I'm going to the dentist."

"We're going shopping for new gym shoes," Penny and Lilly explained.

"My piano lesson is today," said Daisy. "See you later, Minnie."

So Minnie started home alone. As she walked down the sidewalk, she saw Becky hiding behind a tree. Minnie's heart began to thump.

"Nah, nah, nah, Skinny Minnie, Skinny Minnie," Becky yelled. She jumped out from behind the tree and knocked Minnie's schoolbooks on the ground.

I have to be as brave as Fifi, Minnie thought to herself as she picked up her books. She stood up straight and tall and looked Becky right in the eyes.

"You stop bothering me, Becky," Minnie said.

"Make me!" Becky answered, putting her hands on her hips.

Minnie looked at Becky and remembered all her friends' funny ideas. She imagined Becky covered with sand, stuck in a hole full of peanut butter — or maybe up in a tree!

Minnie started to smile. Her smile grew into a great big grin. She started to giggle. And suddenly — she forgot to be scared!

"What's so funny?" Becky demanded.

"You are!" Minnie said.

"Am not!" Becky yelled. She made a terrible face.

"You are, too," Minnie chuckled. "You can't scare me anymore!" Then Minnie stopped laughing and said, "You know, Becky, I think you're kind of silly because you could have real friends, but you'd rather make people afraid of you instead."

Suddenly, Becky started to cry. "No one likes me. I just want someone to pay attention to me!"

Before Minnie could answer, Becky ran away.

Minnie watched her go. "I think I know just what to do next," she said to herself.

When Minnie got home, Fifi was waiting for her.

"Oh, Fifi, you gave me such a good idea yesterday!" Minnie said.
"And it really worked! Here's a treat for being such a great dog!"

Fifi didn't know what Minnie meant, but she liked the crunchy dog
biscuit Minnie gave her!

That night, Minnie called Daisy, Clarabelle, Penny, and Lilly. "Meet
me at the park tomorrow," she said. "I have a surprise!"

Then she made one last, secret phone call.

The next day, Daisy, Clarabelle, Penny, and Lilly hurried to the park.
"Where is Minnie?" Clarabelle asked.
"What do you think her surprise is?" Penny wondered out loud.
"Well, I just hope Becky doesn't show up and ruin it, whatever it is,"
Daisy said.

"Don't look now," Lilly said. "But there's Becky — and she's with Minnie!"

"Oh, no," Daisy groaned. "Here we go again!"

"Hi, everybody," Minnie said. "I asked Becky to play with us today."

"Hi," Becky said softly.

Everyone was very quiet for a minute.

"I'm sorry I threw sand at you the other day, Penny," Becky said. "And I'm sorry for being mean to Clarabelle and Lilly and Daisy, too. I don't want to be a bully anymore," she told them. "I'd rather be your friend."

"Well, that's great, Becky!" Daisy said.
"It will be more fun to be friends," said Penny.
"Absolutely!" Lilly and Clarabelle agreed.
"Well, what are we waiting for? Let's play!" Minnie exclaimed.
Soon all the girls were swooping high into the air on the swings.

When it was time to go home, Penny, Clarabelle, Lilly, Daisy, and Minnie gathered to leave. Becky hesitated for a minute. Then Minnie turned and waved to her.

"Come on, Becky!" Minnie called. "What are you waiting for?"

Soon Becky was walking down the sidewalk arm-in-arm with her new friends, making plans for what they would do tomorrow.